Alan MacDonald
Illustrated by Paul Hess

PEACHTREE
ATLANTA

Once, there were some animals who lived on a farm in a humble, tumble-down barn. One of them was a pig called Peggoty.

Peggoty was a polite, kind-hearted pig. But she was rather proud of her looks, and she spent hours admiring her reflection in the duck pond. She believed herself to be the prettiest, pinkest, most perfect pig in all the world.

One morning, some lambs passed the farmyard gate on their way to the fields. Peggoty was gazing at herself in the duck pond, as usual.

The lambs were very pleased with their new woolly coats and hadn't yet learned any manners. They stopped to stare at her.

"Ugly ol' pig. You're pink and fat, and you're baaaald, too," they bleated.

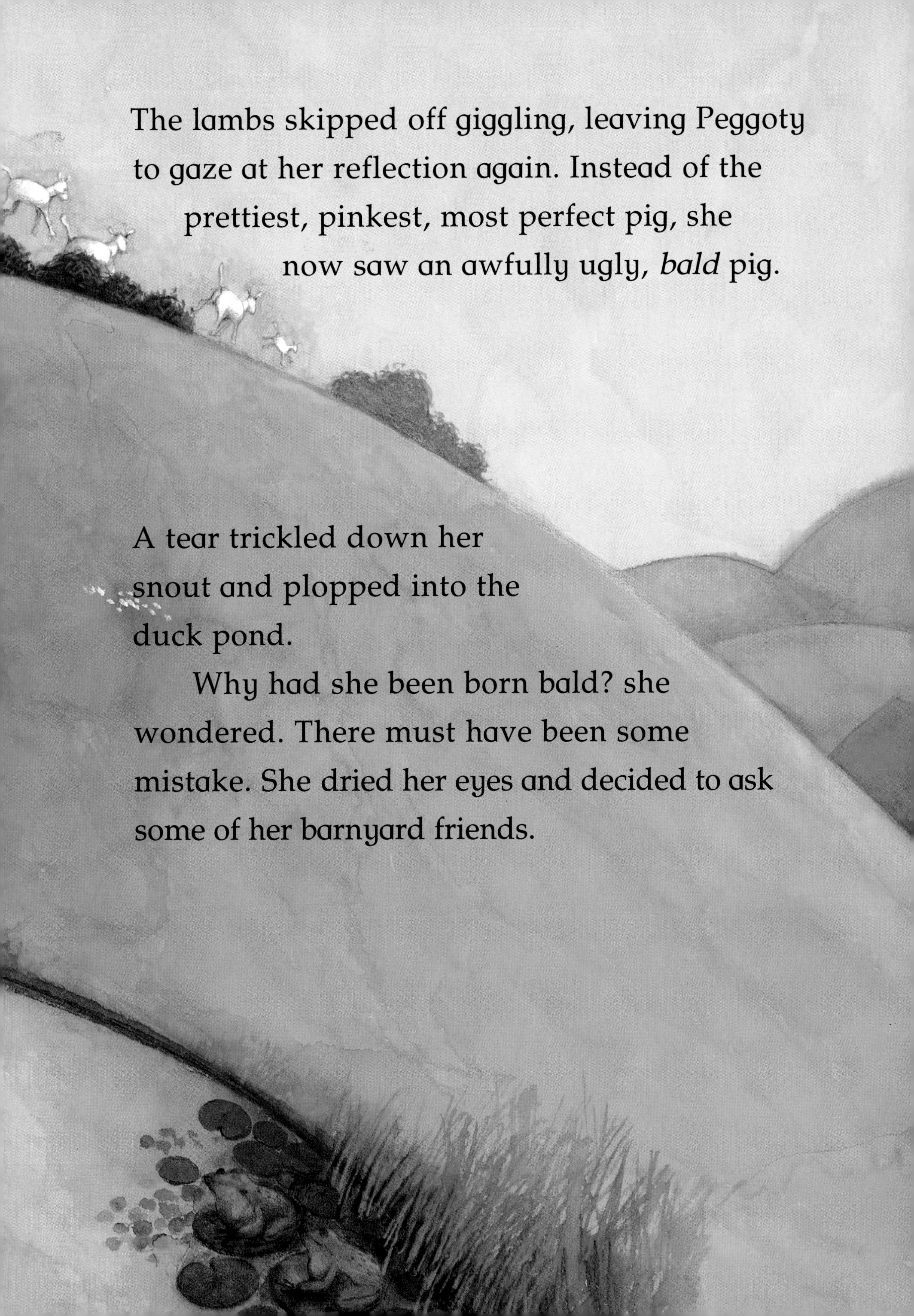

The lambs skipped off giggling, leaving Peggoty to gaze at her reflection again. Instead of the prettiest, pinkest, most perfect pig, she now saw an awfully ugly, *bald* pig.

A tear trickled down her snout and plopped into the duck pond.

Why had she been born bald? she wondered. There must have been some mistake. She dried her eyes and decided to ask some of her barnyard friends.

She found the old horse munching hay in the barn.

"Excuse me," said Peggoty, most politely, "but could you tell me why I am bald?"

"Bald? Ah yes," the old horse said, clearing his throat. "The reason you're bald is that you have no mane," he replied.

"And please," asked Peggoty, "is that what makes me so awfully ugly?"

"Why, of course," nickered the horse. "There is no finer thing in all the world than a glossy and galloping mane."

"I see," said Peggoty. "Thank you."

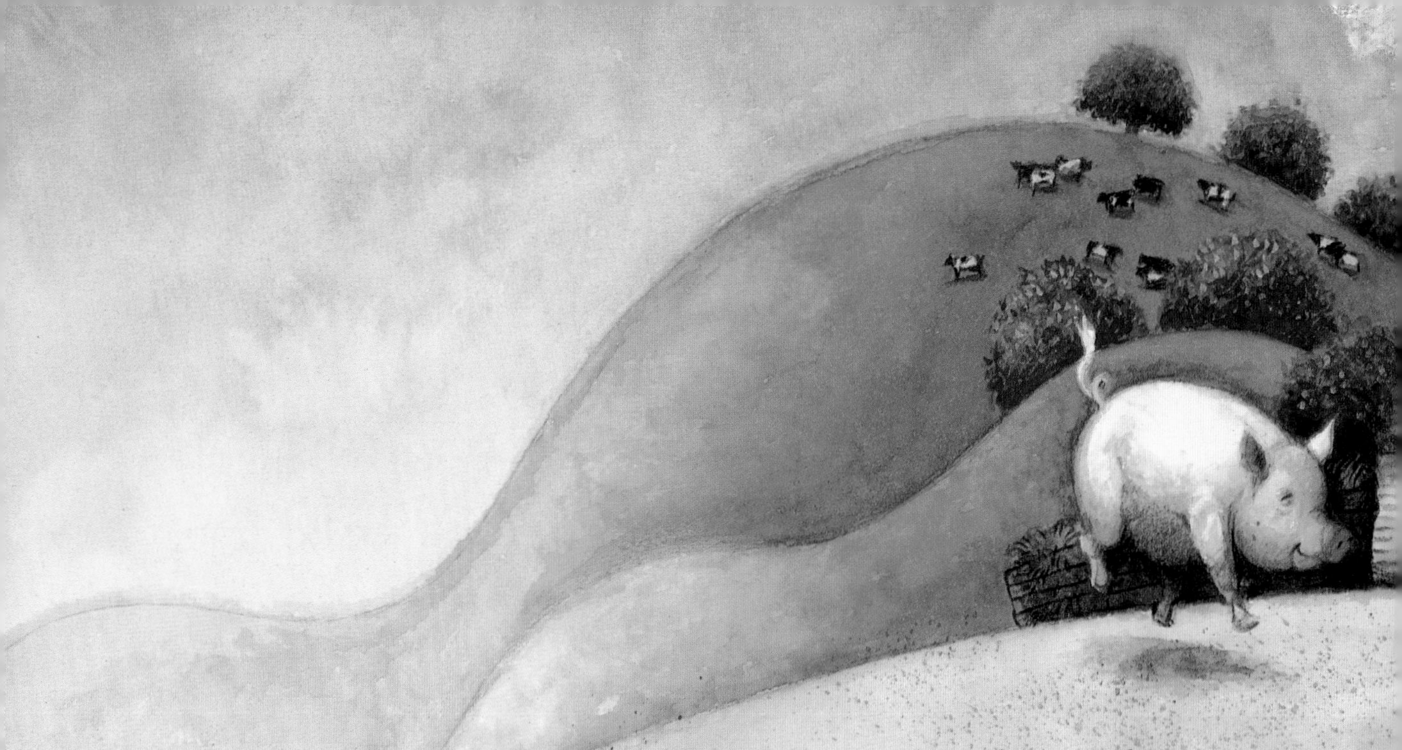

Peggoty trotted into the barnyard, where she spotted the marmalade cat, curled up in a sunny spot.

"Excuse me," said Peggoty, most politely, "but do you know why I am bald?"

The marmalade cat opened one eye and looked at Peggoty. "The reason you're bald is that you're wearing no fur," she replied.

Peggoty nodded sadly. "And is that what makes me so awfully ugly?"

"Of course," purred the cat. "There is no finer thing in the world than lickable, tickable fur."

"I see," said Peggoty. "Thank you."

For the rest of that day Peggoty hid herself from the other animals. It was after dark when she returned to the humble, tumble-down barn. Only the moon was out.

"Oh luminous moon," sighed Peggoty. "Why was I born so bald and awfully ugly?"

To her great surprise, a voice replied. "The reason you're bald is that you have no fabulous feathers to flaunt."

Peggoty looked up. It wasn't the moon talking after all. It was the singing cock on the roof.

"Can you help me?" asked Peggoty, most politely. "I've asked everyone why I'm bald and awfully ugly. And they say it's because I haven't got a glossy and galloping mane or lickable, tickable fur, not to mention fabulous feathers to flaunt. But I don't see what I can do about it."

The cock strutted back and forth on the crest of the roof.

"It would indeed be a strange and wonderful sight if a pig could grow feathers," the cock crowed.

Suddenly Peggoty had an idea. Without thanking the singing cock or bidding it goodnight, she trotted into the barn.

All that night, while the other animals slept, strange rustling and scuffling sounds came from Peggoty's corner.

P
P

When the first sunlight crept into the barn, the cock crowed and the animals stretched and yawned and shuffled out into the yard.

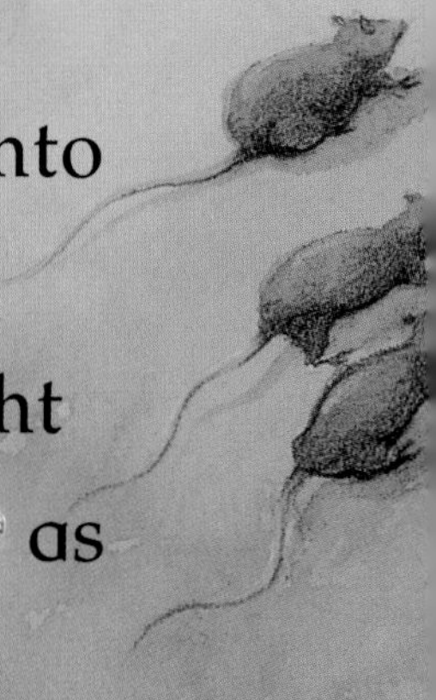

Everyone stared at Peggoty. Overnight she had grown hair—golden locks of hair as curly as a pig's tail.

Peggoty tossed her head proudly and paraded in front of them.

Just then, the young lambs passed by the gate, following their mothers up to the fields.

"Look at the pig!" shouted one. "What's she got on her head?"

"The pig is wearing a wig!" they cried.
They all crowded around the gate, bleating and giggling at poor Peggoty.

"The pig in a wig! The pig in a wig!" they chorused.

Peggoty's pink face turned red. She spun around and fled up the hill. She didn't stop running until she reached the big farmhouse at the top.

There she crept into the shadow of the wall and wept. Tears ran down her plump cheeks, and the straw wig lay crooked and crumpled on her head.

"Waah, waah!" a voice wailed nearby.

Peggoty sniffled and listened. It was coming from the farmhouse.

"Hush, hush, my darling! Don't cry, my precious," another voice sang.

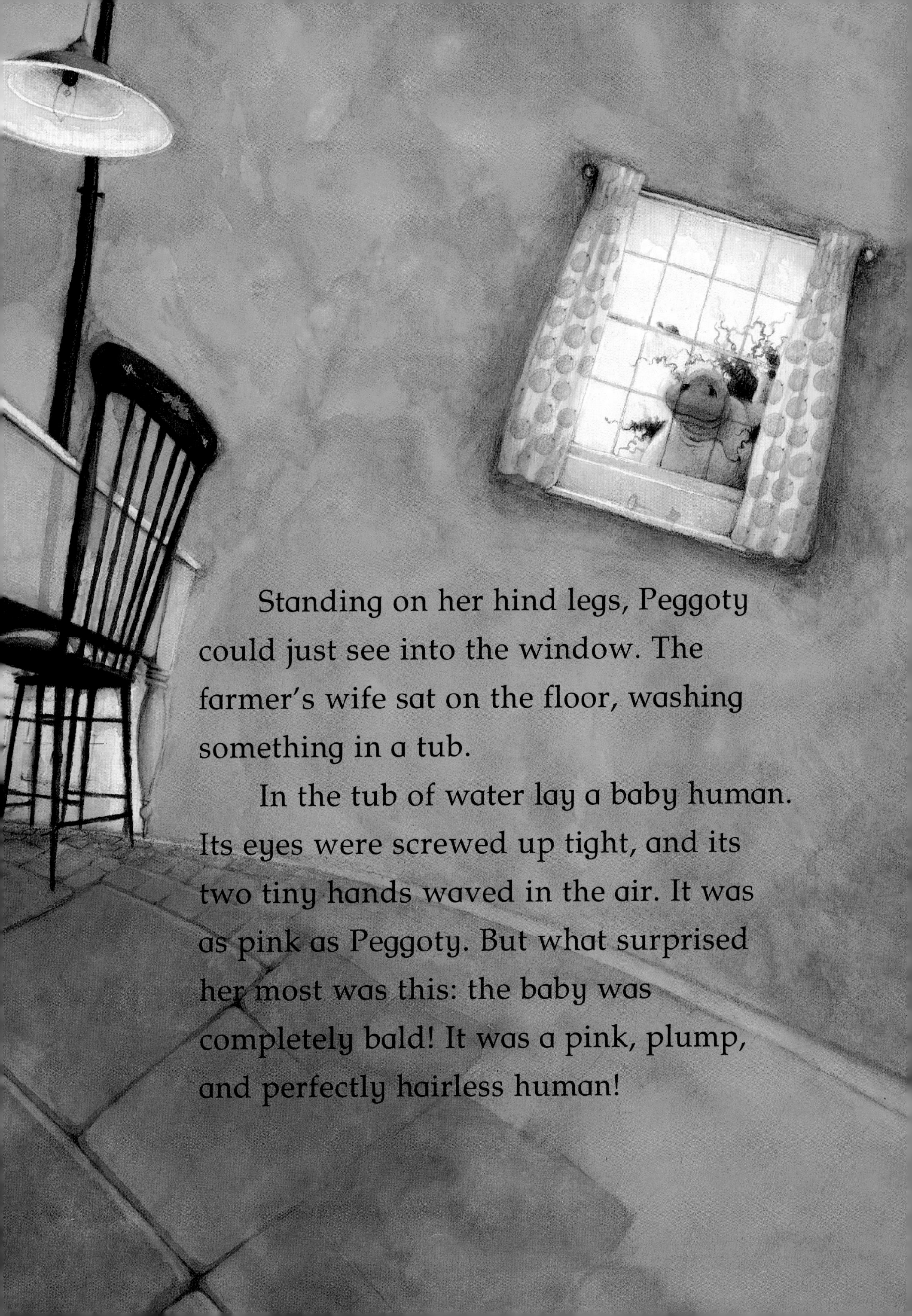

Standing on her hind legs, Peggoty could just see into the window. The farmer's wife sat on the floor, washing something in a tub.

In the tub of water lay a baby human. Its eyes were screwed up tight, and its two tiny hands waved in the air. It was as pink as Peggoty. But what surprised her most was this: the baby was completely bald! It was a pink, plump, and perfectly hairless human!

The farmer's wife tickled the baby's round tummy. "You're beautiful. My beautiful angel," she cooed.

The baby began to gurgle and giggle.

Peggoty pressed her face against the glass, smiling back.

At that moment the farmer's wife looked up and saw the bedraggled, bewigged face at her window.

"HELP!" she screamed. "A horrible, hairy monster!"

Peggoty fell over backward with fright. The crooked and crumpled wig fell off. She left it in the mud and galloped through the gate and back down the hill.

That night, Peggoty told her story to the other animals in the humble, tumble-down barn.

"And so," she concluded, "if you are hairy, humans think you are a horrible monster. But if you are bald," and here she blushed modestly, "they call you an angel."

"And they say you are beautiful," she added, holding up her head a little higher.

Peggoty has never worn a wig since that day. And she doesn't believe that the finest thing in all the world is a glossy and galloping mane, or lickable, tickable fur, or fabulous feathers to flaunt.

She thinks that pigs are born just perfect.

Published by
PEACHTREE PUBLISHERS, LTD.
494 Armour Circle NE
Atlanta, Georgia 30324

www.peachtree-online.com

First published in Great Britain in 1998 by Macdonald Young Books, an imprint of Wayland Publishers Ltd., Hove, East Sussex

First United States edition published in 1999 by Peachtree Publishers, Ltd.

Printed and bound in Belgium

10 9 8 7 6 5 4 3 2 1
First Edition

Library of Congress Cataloging-in-Publication Data

MacDonald, Alan, 1958-
The pig in a wig / Alan MacDonald; illustrated by Paul Hess.
p. cm.
Summary: Peggoty the pig feels ugly when the other animals tell her she needs fur, a mane, or feathers, but then she sees the farmer's baby and learns that there is also beauty in being hairless.
ISBN 1-56145-197-5
[1. Pigs—Fiction. 2. Domestic animals—Fiction. 3. Beauty, Personal—Fiction. 4. Self-acceptance—Fiction.] I. Hess, Paul, ill. II. Title.
PZ7.M4784174Pi 1999
[E]—dc21 98-51318
CIP
AC